教研组成员

顾问　王　奇
组长　黄晓菲
成员　盛　莹　叶洪杰

托福听力满分攻略

Tips for Acing the
TOEFL Listening

澜大教育集团托福教研组　编

中国科学技术大学出版社

内 容 简 介

　　本书是一本介绍托福听力考试题型及考查要点的备考书籍,详细介绍了托福听力考试评分标准,使考生对托福听力考试有完整的认知。全书分为6个章节,每个章节都选取了一些具有代表性的托福听力考试真题,并对其进行了详细的分析和解释,包括具体的考点、要点和答题技巧等。

　　本书旨在帮助托福考生正确认识托福听力,提高对听力的理解能力和应试技巧,在托福备考过程中达到事半功倍的效果。

图书在版编目(CIP)数据

托福听力满分攻略/澜大教育集团托福教研组编. —合肥:中国科学技术大学出版社,2023.10

ISBN 978-7-312-05755-7

Ⅰ. 托… Ⅱ. 澜… Ⅲ. TOEFL—听说教学—自学参考资料 Ⅳ. H319.9

中国国家版本馆 CIP 数据核字(2023)第 151187 号

托福听力满分攻略
TUOFU TINGLI MANFEN GONGLÜE

出版	中国科学技术大学出版社
	安徽省合肥市金寨路 96 号,230026
	http://press.ustc.edu.cn
	https://zgkxjsdxcbs.tmall.com
印刷	安徽省瑞隆印务有限公司
发行	中国科学技术大学出版社
开本	787 mm×1092 mm　1/16
印张	5.5
字数	107 千
版次	2023 年 10 月第 1 版
印次	2023 年 10 月第 1 次印刷
定价	30 元

前　言

　　本书是一本针对托福听力考试的备考书籍,主要介绍了托福听力考试中常见的题目类型和解题技巧。托福听力是一项考察英语听力能力和学术知识的测试,其中涉及很多复杂的语法结构和专业术语,这给很多考生带来了不小的困难。有时候,即使我们能听清每一个单词,也不一定能理解句子的意思,那些长长的句子就像一团团杂乱的毛线球,让我们感到无从下手。

　　高中的时候,我准备出国深造,因此需要参加托福考试。我从小虽然英语成绩还不错,但一直习惯于"先看题目—后听听力—再做题"的考试模式。后来,我在准备托福听力的过程中发现,托福听力是"先盲听—记笔记—后做题"的模式。密集的信息就像机关枪一样,刚写下一个单词,重要信息已经错过两三句了,导致我根本抓不住重点。为了考到理想的分数,我就下苦工夫,花费一整年的时间听写句子,听写的话题范围从VOA到BBC,强迫自己一定要听懂每一句话,最终的结果是有效的,但过程也是痛苦、枯燥的。后来,当我和我的美国舍友闲聊起英文听力学习时,她问我:"你现在还在逐字逐句地听吗? 我们只是把最主要的信息提取出来而已,你让我重复新闻里说的每个单词、每个句子,我也是不太可能做到的。"这是我第一次意识到,我之前练习听力的方式是错误的,我以为需要听懂每个单词才能听懂整个句子。在这之后,我开始探索英文句子的结构和逻辑,逐渐明白英文句子是一个有层次、有重点、有关系的整体。当我开始真正掌握英文句子的破解方法时,我豁然开朗了,曾经晦涩难懂的句子突然变得清晰起来,就算在课堂上,教授说再多的专业术语,我都能抓住重点、轻松应对,不再惧怕任何听力内容。

　　后来我成为了一名托福教师,在教授托福的过程中,我发现很多考生都在经历我当年经历过的事情,希望通过本书,能提高考生对听力的理解能力与应试技巧。本书集结了澜大教育集团托福听力教研组盛莹老师和叶洪杰老师的十年教学经验,希望能帮助考生们攻克托福听力!

黄晓菲

2023 年 4 月

目　　录

第一章　托福听力简介

"得托福听力者得天下"。熟悉托福考试的同学一定知道,听力在托福考试中出现的频率非常高,除了听力模块本身需要考查听力水平以外,写作和口语两个输出模块也会涉及听力理解,所以练好听力尤为重要。

和雅思听力不同的是,托福听力的内容更加学术化,对考生的词汇量要求更高。此外,托福听力是先盲听、记笔记,再看题、做题,因此对考生的记笔记能力、抓重点能力以及瞬间记忆能力的要求也会更高。所以对于一部分不知道该如何记笔记,并且听完就忘的考生来说,攻克听力真的是一项重大的挑战。本书将全面介绍托福听力考点及解题技巧,逐步带领各位考生冲刺托福听力 28 分。

攻克托福听力第一步:了解它!

托福听力考试由 2 个 section 组成:小 section 为 1 篇 conversation 和 1 篇 lecture,大 section 为 1 篇 conversation 和 2 篇 lecture。每篇 conversation 包含 5 道题,音频时长为 2~3 分钟,每篇 lecture 包含 6 道题,音频时长为 5~6 分钟。全场考试共 28 道题。

托福听力答题采用倒计时制,考生必须在规定时间内答完所有题目,倒计时结束时,没有完成的题目自动判错。每道题本身没有答题时间限制,也就是说,考生需要合理规划答题时间。一般来说,大 section 会有 10 分钟的答题时间,小 section 会有 5~6 分钟的答题时间,平均每道题耗时约 36 秒。超出 1 分钟还在纠结的题目需要有所取舍,至少保证有时间完成能够答对的题目。

听力中 conversation 的场景分成两个部分:办公室场景和学生服务场景。办公室场景中,通常讨论的是偏学术性的话题,如某节课上没有听懂的内容或是作业中一些没有弄清楚的理论等。当然也会有部分非学术性讨论,如老师指导学生申请项目资金或学生想要更换考试时间等。学生服务场景的内容相对丰富,往往涉及学生在图书馆、餐厅或生活中遇到的难题,寻求老师探讨解决方案。所以大多数考生觉得 conversation 的内容比较贴近生活,相对好理解。而 lecture 都是模拟学生在大学课堂中听课的场景,所涉及的学科内容较多,包含四个大类,即艺术、生命科学、社会科学和自然科学。其中生命科学考查的频率最高,艺术和自然科学中的天文、地质部分让大多数考生觉得理解困难,所以备考托福听力的同学可以先把这些学科的场景词汇准备起来。

第二章　托福听力考试中的常见问题

1．单词都认识，但是听不懂

如果听单词没有办法迅速理解其意思，本质上就是对单词发音不够熟悉。平时背单词时就要精准掌握单词的发音，可以借助在线字典，模仿单词或短语的发音，直到熟练掌握发音为止。

即使遇到的是专业术语或日常生活学习中较少使用的词汇，也不用费尽心思去背诵其意思。在托福听力考试过程中，通常都会对这类专业术语进行解释，只需要听懂后面解释的内容就好。

2．笔记对答题没有帮助

笔记中如果出现了很多无关紧要的信息，可能表明考生只是听到什么记什么，而不是记下了关键性的单词。记笔记的时候一般以重要的名词、动词和形容词作为有效信息，除此之外，类似 in、the、of 等都可以不用记下来。一般情况下，一个句子只需要记 2～4 个单词就可以帮助考生回忆出整个句子的大意,如果记下的单词并不能帮助考生回忆出这个句子的内容,则很有可能记录的是无效信息或是没有记全最关键的词汇。

3. 短句能听懂,长句跟不上

其实考生之所以能听懂短句是因为平时听到太多次了。例如"How are you? I'm fine, and you?"考生无需在脑海里处理这段信息就能立刻反应过来。但是长句的内容是考生平时很少用到的句子,再加上一些生词,理解起来就有些困难。

这时候需要加强对句子反应力的练习,长的句子可以试着听两遍,记2～3个关键词,如果看着自己记的单词也无法复述句子大意的话,就直接看文本精读句子,理解大意后再听一遍,再试着记关键词,看看是否真正听清并理解句子的意思。

4. 文章"听懂"了,答案都不对

这个时候的"听懂"只是考生自以为听懂了,但其实并没有真正理解句子的意思,很有可能只是听了个大概,然后看着选项感觉意思对了,就下手选了。真正的听懂要能在脑海里搭建出答案句和正确选项之间的逻辑关系,且是快速搭建起来的。因为托福听力考试的题目除了考查直接的细节,还会考查考生能否真正理解听力材料中相关人物说话的目的,所以题目经常会出现"why mention"这样的字眼,这时候更多考查的是逻辑方面的内容。

5. 听着听着会走神，怎么办

听一大段信息会走神，这是人之常情。我们要训练的就是循序渐进地听材料。

平时自我练习的时候，在走神的地方就可以暂停，分析走神的原因，有可能是没有听懂，有可能是受生词的影响，有可能是自己的状态不好，找到原因之后再针对性地解决问题。

如果因为句子太长没有听懂，暂停之后，试着把前面的内容大致复述一下，再重听一下暂停的地方，这样就可以清楚地了解是否是因为句子太长而走神。如果是，本质上也是因为不理解句子主干，被从句的信息干扰，导致不想听或听不下去，解决方案就是加强对长句的反应力，抓好主干，理解句意后也就不容易走神了。如果是因为自己本身的耐力不够强，听着听着有些困倦了，那同样也可以暂停，设置好自己听听力的停顿时间，循序渐进，把暂停的地方逐次多听半分钟并复述之前的内容，直到自己适应听力文本的长度。

众所周知，除了上课时消化、理解老师教授的常见考点，掌握一些做题技巧，坚持刷题保持做题感觉以外，想要达到"质"的飞跃，提升听力整体水平，必不可少的一个步骤就是精听。

托福听力的"精听"到底该怎么做？推荐以下两种方法！

第一种——单句听抄。

第二种——单句复述。

第一种，适合托福听力得分≤20分的考生。

这个分数段的考生对于听力的整体内容不太理解，或者只理解了小半部分，但是看着自己的笔记时，无法进行有逻辑的梳理，关键考点部分基本就错过了。针对这类考生，可以进行比较"简单粗暴"的单句听抄。

单句听抄步骤：

① 打开 TPO（TOEFL Practice Online）的单句精听功能，反复播放；

② 播放过程不暂停，直到写完整个单句为止；

③ 整篇听完后，全文精读至理解文章意思，积累生词；

④ 积累本篇文章的相关的背景知识。

注意事项：

① 播放过程不暂停是为了减少点击屏幕的时间，任何点击屏幕的操作都有可能跳转到其他界面从而导致分心，浪费时间。

② 这个分数段需要锻炼的是对单词意思或句子意思的反应力。

如果觉得听抄的时候注意力全放在单词和听写上去了，没有办法理解整个句子的意思。没有关系，后续的精读会有足够的时间去理解文章。大脑是个神奇的器官，在阅读的时候，停顿和语调其实是会自动浮现出来的，只是自己可能没有意识到。

③ 坚持一段时间后，考生会发现自己对句子的反应力有了进一步提升，之后，就可以采用第二种"精听"的方法进行练习。

第二种，适合托福听力得分≥20分的同学。

这个分数段的考生对于听力的整体理解达到了70%以上，能够抓住某些重点信息，但并非能完全理解听力内容，且对于一些需要转换思路的选项理解得不够透彻，所以更需要锻炼的是听到句子之后，即刻反应出大致的中文意思的能力。

单句复述步骤：

① 打开TPO的单句精听功能，眼睛看向别处，手指操作；

② 听一句，复述其中文意思，直到整篇听完；

③ 如果句子听不懂，无法即刻反应中文意思，则播放两遍；

④ 两遍之后还不理解，直接看文本并理解中文意思；

⑤ 不懂的句子再放一遍，模仿跟读两遍；

⑥ 在精听复述的过程中，积累生词，多次复习。

以上两种方法都能帮助到各阶段的考生，考生可以根据自己的实际情况进行微调，但大致做法都是一致的。要记住，任何方法都是纸上谈兵，都要落实到"行动＋坚持"上。任何科目都不是通过临时抱佛脚和刷题就能短期提分的，即使提了分也多半是运气成分居多。为了长远考虑，每天坚持一点点，进步一点点，才会有"质"的飞跃，突破"瓶颈"！

第三章　托福听力常考题型

和雅思听力相比,托福听力的题型相对单一,全部都是选择题。其中单选最多,辅之以多选和一些表格题。多选部分会有 4 选 2、5 选 3 等题目出现,表格题可以细分为判断题、分类题以及排序题。单选、多选、表格题目难度依次递增,出现的频率依次递减。托福听力分数在不同阶段目标不同,可以分批次攻克这些题目类型。托福官方将这些题目分成以下 3 大考查方向,7 种题型类别。

- Basic Comprehension Questions

① Gist-Content

② Gist-Purpose

③ Detail

- Pragmatic Understanding Questions

④ Understanding the Function of What Is Said

⑤ Understanding the Speaker's Attitude

- Connecting Information Questions

⑥ Understanding Organization/Connecting Content

⑦ Making Inferences

接下来,我们分别看一下每种题型的考查要点和常见提问方式。

1. 内容主旨题

内容主旨题(Gist-Content Questions)主要考查考生对文章中心思想的归纳总结能力,考生解题时可以尝试用一句话归纳文章大意再和选项匹配。内容主旨题的常见提问方式如下。

(1) Gist-Content (Lecture)

- What are the speakers mainly discussing?
- What is the main topic of the lecture?
- What is the lecture mainly about?
- What aspect of X does the professor mainly discuss?

(2) Gist-Content (Conversation)

- What is the conversation mainly about?
- What are the speakers mainly discussing?

2. 目的主旨题

目的主旨题(Gist-Purpose Questions)需要考生理解对话或讲座的目的而非主要内容。

考生往往需要更多关注音频开头部分的表述。另外,此类问题主要出现在对话中,偶尔也会出现在讲座音频中。目的主旨题的常见提问方式如下。

- Why does the student visit the professor?
- Why does the student visit the registrar's office?
- Why did the professor ask to see the student?
- Why does the professor explain...?

3. 细节题

细节题(Detail Questions)主要考查对文章主旨有支持作用的重要细节内容,如举例、解释、原因、结果等,一些特别细枝末节的内容一般不会考查。值得一提的是,有时候看似与主旨无关的题外话出现在 conversation 中,也有可能被考查,所以考生们要小心 conversation 中的附加信息。细节题的常见提问方式如下。

- According to the professor，what is one way that X can affect Y?
- What is X?
- What resulted from the invention of the X?
- According to the professor，what is the main problem with the X theory?

4. 句子功能题

句子功能题(Understanding the Function of What Is Said)往往在重听题中出现,考查考生对说话人真正意图或意思的理解,所以往往需要选择言外之意。句子功能题的常见提问方式如下。

- What does the professor imply when he says this?（replay）
- Why does the student say this?（replay）
- What does the professor mean when she says this?（replay）

5. 态度题

态度题（Understanding the Speaker's Attitude Questions）主要考查学生对说话人态度的判断能力。需要结合上下文判断说话人对前面提及的人物、理论等持积极、消极还是中性的态度。态度题的常见提问方式如下。

- What is the professor's attitude toward the expert on the television program?
- What can be inferred about the student?
- What is the professor's attitude toward X?
- What is the professor's opinion of X?
- What can be inferred about the student when she says this?（replay）
- What does the woman mean when she says this?（replay）

可以发现，态度题有可能出现在重听题里面，另外有些态度题的提问方式会类似于推断题，题目中含有"infer"这样的字眼，考生要注意区分。

6. 连接内容题

连接内容题（Connecting Content Questions）主要考查学生是否能够将音频中听到的内

容联系成一个整体,理清各事物之间的逻辑关系,了解事情发展的正确顺序等。连接信息题常见的问法如下。

- What is the likely outcome of doing procedure X before procedure Y?
- What can be inferred about X?
- What does the professor imply about X?

连接题往往以表格的形式出现,可以把它细分为3个类别:判断型、分类型、排序型。

(1) 判断型

这类题目要求考生判断某一信息表达是否和文中一致,一般来说音频中会有相应的信号句,如"what happens is"。考生在听到相关信号句之后要注意记录相关核心名词。如果来不及记录的话,先听懂整个句子。解题过程中还可以借助相关规律判断,一般来说"Yes"的个数会比"No"略多。例如:

The professor mentions parts of the process involved in the formation of Lechuguilla Cave. Indicate which of the statements below describe part of the process.

	Yes	No
Gypsum residue accumulated to form decorative structures.		
Gas generated by bacteria reacted with gypsum deposits.		
Hydrogen sulfide gas mixed with underground water.		
Acid dissolved parts of the limestone.		
Bacteria fed on underground oil.		
Flowing surface water enlarged the cracks in the limestone.		

(2) 分类型

在听音频的时候,如果发现音频中明确出现两个不同的类别(往往是一组反义词,如

active 和 passive），要记录清楚这两个类别的异同点。如果有漏记的情况出现，不用慌张，通常可以将其中一方的特点取非成为另一方的特点。例如：

According to the professor what is true about the hero in chanson poetry and the in romance poetry? Click in the correct box for each phrase.

		Chanson Hero	Romance Hero
1	Is admired for loyalty to country		
2	Engages in conflict for adventure		
3	Is willing to face extreme dangers to protect the lord		
4	Is concerned with individual improvement		

(3) 排序型

解答此类题目时是有迹可循的。需要排序的题目，在原文中往往会出现大量表示先后顺序的连接词。同学们需要尽量将步骤记录清楚，优先考虑记录动词。答题时可按照记录的动词进行排序。另外音频中的内容一般符合一件事情发展的合理逻辑，如果实在没有记录清楚，可以结合逻辑合理性进行推断。例如：

The professor describes three sections the art history paper should contain. Place them in the order in which they should appear in the paper.

Click on a phrase. Then drag it to the space where it belongs.

1	
2	
3	

Answer Choices

a. Analysis of the design elements the artist uses

b. Discussion of the meaning of the artwork

c. Summary of the appearance of the artwork

7. Inference Questions 推断题

推断题考查考生根据上下文内容,听出说话人言外之意的能力。考生需要结合语境进行推论。脱离语境,仅凭一句话下定论往往很容易出错。另外,推断题也有可能出现在重听题当中。推断题的常见提问方式如下。

- What does the professor imply about...?

- What will the student probably do next?

- What can be inferred about...?

- What does the professor imply when he says this? (replay)

第四章 托福听力常见考点

1. 对话考点

在托福听力对话中遇到的各类场景,其实都是将来在美国校园生活中会真实遇到的场景,主要涉及生活类对话和学术类对话。无论是哪种场景,都需要考生在短时间内抓取对话中最重要的信息点,明确说话者的目的,理解其背后的含义。

(1) "Mainly discuss"或学生与教授的对话

通常,对话题目的第一题有两种问法,分别是 Why does the woman go to see the man/professor? 和 What do the speakers mainly discuss? 如果 mainly discuss 的内容需要听完整段对话之后才能判断文章整体说了什么,一般来说该音频中没有明显的信号句。但是,如果是问学生为什么要来找教授或教授为什么要来找学生,那么音频中就会有比较明显的信号句。值得注意的是,信号句出现的位置是不固定的,有可能在音频的开头部分、中间部分甚至是音频的结尾部分。

① 学生找教授

【经典信号句】

- I was wondering...

- I just want to...

- I'd like to know...

- I have some questions about...

- I actually came here to find out if you're interested in...

- I've been thinking about...

- That's why I come by/stop by...

- I'm trying to...

TPO-71/Conversation 2

☞ Why does the man go to see the professor?

A. To get the professor's opinion about the name of a magazine

B. To ask for the professor's assistance in producing a magazine

C. To discuss the quality of writing in a student magazine

D. To explain why a previous attempt to start a magazine failed

文本：

Professor：Sounds great. I like that diversity of content.

Student：I'm really glad you say that because I actually came here to find out if you're interested in being our faculty advisor.

在这段话中，学生使用 I actually came here to find out 说出自己的目的，询问教授是否愿意当杂志的指导老师。

答案 B

TPO-70/Conversation 1

☞ Why does the student go to the student activities office?

A. To register for an upcoming ski trip

B. To obtain information about a previous ski trip

C. To help organize a school ski trip

D. To suggest a location for a future ski trip

文本：

Student：Hi，is this where I find out about school trips?

Employee：Sure，it is. How can I help You?

Student：Well，I'm looking for information about a ski trip.

Employee：Oh，yeah，We just scheduled one for next，month. We haven't even had time to advertise it yet，so you'll be the first to sign up well actually.

Student：Well，actually，I wanted to know about an old ski trip from about 7 years ago，my brother went on it，and he still talks about the wonderful hotel. I think it was a ski lodge that they stayed at.

在这段话中，学生先是提出想了解 ski trip 的信息，Employee 错认为学生想了解最新的 ski trip。但其实不是，经过确认之后，学生说 actually，I wanted to know about 7 年前的 ski trip，所以对应选项 B 中的 previous ski trip。

答案　B

② 教授找学生

【经典信号句】

• So，Mary，you got my email. What do you think?

• How can I help?

• What can I do for you?

• I'm just concerned that…

• I'm just a little unclear about…

• The reason I wanted to talk to you was that…

TPO-61/Conversation 1

☞ Why did the professor make an appointment with the student?

A. To discuss a book they both read

B. To give her suggestions on her writing style

C. To compliment her essay form

D. To talk about the content of her essay

文本：

Professor：Alright，Karen．I'm glad you stopped by for our appointment．So we can chat before you write the final draft of your essay．

Student：Is there something wrong? I mean，is there something I forgot?

Professor：Well，you've got the correct essay form and all that．You followed the writing guidelines very well，so there's no problem there．

Student：That's encouraging．Professor…

Professor：I'm just a little unclear about some of the content．You seem to be unsure of what you want to say in a few places．And I want you to take a look at that．

在这段话中，教授先是表扬了学生的 essay 还不错，转而使用 I'm just a little unclear about 的信号句带出想要讨论一下学生 essay 的内容。

答案　D

(2) 针对问题提出解决方案

通常，在对话中，考生需要学会抓取教授提出的解决方案，解决方案也有两种：一种是暂时性的，有可能会被拒绝；另一种是最终的解决方案，通常出现在对话的最后部分。在这些解决方案中，特别要注意教授针对学生的作业、论文或者项目提出的几点建议，有可能会考查多选题。

【经典信号句】

• It's strongly recommended that…

• I highly recommend you talk to…

• Don't forget to…

- You might want to...

- I suggest...

- I think you should/can/could...

- It would be interesting to...

例题

TPO-55/Conversation 2

☞ What does the adviser suggest that the student do? Choose two answers.

A. Make up the work she has missed

B. Contact the registrar's office

C. Apologize to an art history professor

D. Drop the Islamic art course

文本:

Advisor：Well，it's strongly recommended that students meet with their advisors early in the semester，and now you can see why. But there's no real harm done. However，don't forget to file a formal withdrawal from introduction to art history with the registrar's office by Friday，when the withdrawal period ends. And you might want to apologize to professor Miller as well.

Student：Oh，I'll definitely make an appointment of dropping by his office to explain what happened. I was just so focused on getting admitted into the Islamic art course and so happy when professor Campbell said I could take it that I kind forgot about everything else.

在这段对话中，教授使用 don't forget to 和 you might want to 这两个信号句带出两件建议学生做的事，且对应答案句里的原词原句。

答案　BC

例题

TPO-58/Conversation 1

☞ Why does the woman suggest that the student call the curator's office? Choose two answers.

A. To find out if he can work there

B. To get more information about the sculpture garden

C. To apologize for causing a problem at the museum

D. To learn what background he will need to become a curator

文本：

Employee：Well，there are museum jobs that don't involve interacting with the public，you know，working behind the scenes. You could help set up exhibits，document new acquisitions，maybe work as an assistant to the curators office，it wouldn't hurt to ask about other opportunities there.

Student：Would you call and ask if I could，like you said work with the curator? I've only met her a couple of times but she...

Employee：You know，I think you should call. Tell the curator what you told me and ask if they could use any help.

Student：What if she says no.

Employee：You could still ask for information that might help you in the future. Like what courses you should take and what kind of work experience is necessary to become a curator.

在这段话中，Employee 使用 you should call 和 you could still ask for 作为信号句带出后面的建议。

答案　AD

TPO-65/Conversation 2

☞ What is the professor's suggestion for the student's first paper?

A. An essay comparing two plays by Chekhov

B. A paper on plays written by playwrights from different time periods

C. An essay focusing on the characteristics of contemporary drama

D. A paper on *The Cryptogram* and its influence on contemporary playwrights

文本：

Professor：This is a course on modern drama and that is what we're reading. I mean if you're interested in contemporary dramatists and you can if you want to write your first paper on a contemporary playwright but only if comparison with the work of an earlier playwrights. I think that would be a good exercise and it might even help you resolve some of the problems we talked about today.

在这段话中，教授使用 you can if you want to write 带出学生写论文的建议：与之前的 playwright 作对比。

答案　B

TPO-66/Conversation 2

☞ What advice does the woman give the man? Choose two answers.

A. To reduce his course load this semester

B. To pay more attention to his spending habits

C. To postpone looking for a job

D. To start taking public transportation

文本：

Student：Well If I got a job, I'd certainly have a little more spending money. And that would show my parents I'm managing on my own.

Professor：But what's your course load this semester? If you have more than four courses, you might want to work on your budget and monitor your spending rather than get a job for now.

Student：Well I have four courses, but one is biology. And there's a 3 hour lab each week. So it's really like a 5th course.

Professor：You wanna think about it then，maybe try to work on your budget and spending for a month and see how you're doing. If you're still strapped for cash，but you're keeping up with all your course work，then you could try to find a job.

在这段对话中，教授使用 you might want to work on 和 maybe try to work on 强调了两遍先注意自己的日常花销，再去考虑找工作的事。

答案　BC

(3) 对话里的否定句

在托福听力对话篇章中，针对说话者提出的建议、猜想、意见等，都会有回应同意与否。在同意的情况下，考生会有意识地记下关键性的要点。但要记住的是，说话者表达不同意之后提出来的理由是更加重要的。由于中英文的说话习惯、发音特点和叙述风格，考生对于否定句的出现不够敏感，但这恰恰是托福听力考查学生是否真正理解对话的意图。

【经典信号句】

• not/no：didn't，weren't，can't，won't...

• 带有否定词前缀的信号词：dis-（disprove），un-（unhappy），im-（impossible），in-（incorrect）...

• 缺点缺陷：problem，weakness，limitation，...

TPO-56/Conversation 1

☞ What does the professor imply about studying business?

A. It will improve the student's chances of being accepted into graduate school.

B. It may not be a wise choice for the student.

C. It could help the student clarify her career goals.

D. There may be fewer jobs in this field than the student thinks.

文本：

Professor: Okay，studying something like great businesses preparation，of course，especially for people who already know their career goals，but for those who don't... Well，what's yours? What are your goals?

Student: I have no idea.

Professor: So for you，perhaps it's not the best option.

Student: That's a good point.

在这段对话中，教授询问学生是否知道自己的 career goals，学生直言自己也不知道，所以教授使用 So for you，perhaps it's not the best option 这个否定句来说明对于学生来说，选 business 并非一个很好的选择。

答案　B

例题

TPO-60/Conversation 2

☞ Why is the professor not aware that Parents' Weekend is scheduled for the end of this week?

A. He thought it had been cancelled this year.

B. It is usually scheduled later in the year.

C. It was not listed in the official academic schedule.

D. He misread the academic calendar.

文本：

Professor: Look，the film was required viewing from French 207，then since I couldn't schedule a one hour film during our regular fifty minute class. I know it's short notice，but I'll only have the film for a few days.

Student: It's just that I already told my parents...

Professor: You know，Parent's Weekend isn't listed on the academic calendar.

Student: That's true.

在这段对话中，教授直接使用 isn't listed on the academic calendar 这个否定的句子来

说明教授并不知道 Parents' Weekend 的存在,对应答案的 not listed in the official academic schedule。

答案　C

TPO-60/Conversation 2

☞ What mistake did the student make?

A. She forgot to pay her housing fee.

B. She did not cancel her telephone service.

C. She failed to clean out her dormitory room.

D. She forgot to return her dormitory key to the housing office.

文本:

Employee:Right. Do you remember making arrangements to have your phone service turned off before you left?

Student:Was I supposed to do that?

Employee:Yeah,you were.

Student:I didn't know that.

Employee:Yeah,it's in the contract.

在这段对话中,学生直接说了 I didn't know that,自己并不知道需要取消自己的 phone service,对应答案里的 did not cancel。

答案　B

(4) 对话里的人物

在对话中,除了说话者两人以外,会在对话内容中提到第三方的人物,这是一种信号,提示考生理解说话者为什么要提到这个人物,提这个人物有什么目的。常见的第三方人物有:friend,brother,sister,parents,niece/nephew,roommate,administrator,advisor,assistant, librarian，president，dean，curator，classmate，volunteer，employer/employee，other professors，some people 以及根据学术内容提到的各种专家学者们，如生物学家、艺术家等。

TPO-66/Conversation 2

☞ What does the man imply about his parents?

A. They are worried about his financial situation.

B. They are not willing to increase his allowance.

C. They do not want him to get a job.

D. They are unhappy that he did not tell them about his problem.

文本：

Employee：You mean you didn't pay your tuition bill?

Student：No，no，I'm okay with the big stuff. I mean I have student loans that pay for most of the tuition，but well it's it's the everyday things that add up.

Employee：Oh. You mean like books，food，things like that.

Student：Yeah. My parents give me an allowance for that stuff，but it's just not enough. I've asked them to increase it even a little，but they think I need to learn to manage on my own.

在这段话中，学生提到了日常花销大，且提到了关键性的第三方人物父母，说父母也不愿意给自己增加多一点点津贴。出现第三方人物的时候要注意快速反应为什么会提到这个人物。

答案　B

TPO-57/Conversation 2

☞ Why does the man need to talk to his sister?

A. To ask her if he can borrow her car

B. To ask her for a ride to Pearson Hall

C. To ask her to bring his student ID card from home

D. To ask her to check out a journal from the language department library

文本:

Librarian:Sure. It's on the other campus in the basement of Pearson Hall across from the listening lab. But I doubt you'll be able to make it over there in time today.

Student:No，especially since I don't have a car but my sister does，and I'm pretty sure she'd let me borrow it.

在这段话中,学生说自己没有车,但是 sister 有,所以提到第三方人物是想说明自己可以向 sister 借车。

答案 A

例题

TPO-58/Conversation 1

☞ What information was included in the report from the museum director?

A. The student spoke with friends when he should have been helping visitors.

B. The student did not give accurate inform at ion to museum visitors.

C. The student arrived late to work on one occasion.

D. The student requested a job in a different part of the museum.

文本:

Student:Hi，I'm Paul Benson.

Employee:Paul Benson. Oh，that's a coincidence. The museum directors sent a fax about you. Your two month review，your job review.

Student:Oh，okay. I guess we can do that first.

Employee:Alright. Let's see，overall you're doing a good job I have to stress that，but the director didn't know that you invited friends over during working hours instead of greeting visitors and answering questions about the outdoor sculpture garden，like you are supposed to. You talked with your friends.

Student：It was only that one time and they just showed up, I did not invite them. I strained it out with the director.

在这段对话中，Employee 指出学生工作时和朋友聊天了，直接对应选项的原句 spoke with friends，第三方人物就是 friends。

答案　A

(5) 对话里的语气

在托福听力的对话中，由于场景的多样性和对话力求真实，说话者会出现各种各样的语气，包括不耐烦、激动、生气、高兴、遗憾、惋惜、焦虑等。当语气有明显变化时，有可能会考重听题，探讨说话者的目的，为什么要说这句话，说话者暗示（imply）了什么意思．这就要求考生在听的过程中，能快速反应句子真正的含义，而不是停留在字面意思。

 例题

TPO-67/Conversation 1

☞ What does the woman imply about her next-door neighbors?

A. Their kitchen is too dirty for her to use.

B. Their stove is not functioning properly.

C. They do not let other people use their stove.

D. They will be using their kitchen this weekend.

文本：

Supervisor：Couldn't you, like, use a neighbor's stove or something?

Student：Ewww, I don't think so! I mean, the only neighbors I really know well enough to ask are the guys next door. Huh, if you saw the state of that kitchen, you'd understand. I'm not sure I could find the stove under all the mess.

在这段对话中,对于管理员提出的可以借邻居的灶台用,学生发出了嫌弃的 ewww,I don't think so! 紧接着表达自己不会借邻居灶台的理由对应选项中的 too dirty。

答案 A

TPO-62/Conversation 1

☞ How does the student feel about the professor's explanation of simulations?

A. He finds it amusing and interesting.

B. He feels even more confused than before.

C. He is grateful for the clarification.

D. He realizes that he already understands the general concept.

文本:

Student: Yes, yeah. The whole thing about the simulation, would you mind going over that with me again?

Professor: No problem. The main point of the book I was referring to, is that, well, in a post modern world, we live in a world of unreal images of simulations. For example, the things we see on TV become a reality for us, even though they are not in fact real. They are representations, simulations of reality.

Student: Post modern world?

Professor: Right, it came after the modern one.

Student: Gee, thanks a lot.

Professor: No, sorry, you're right. Post modern, well, that's a sticky term that covers a lot of things, let's save that for later. But back to my point about simulation, it leads to hyper realism, a feeling that something is more real than real.

Student: Wow, wow, ah, I'm sorry, but all this is, I just don't get it.

在这段对话中,学生希望教授再解释一遍什么是 simulation,但是教授解释后学生还是不太明白,已经觉得跟不上了,赶忙打断教授的解释,坦言自己还是不太明白这个概念。

答案　B

(6) 对话开头的闲聊

托福听力对话的背景大多都是在美国校园里真实发生的,而音频也尽可能地还原了真实的对话场景。因此,有些音频就会出现一开始说话时并不是直奔主题,而是先寒暄、问候,甚至是抱怨几句之后再步入正题。这些开头的"闲聊"看似无关紧要,但其实也可以出题。在实际考试中,这会出现在第2题的位置,询问这些"闲聊"中的一些信息。这就要求考生在听力开始时马上进入状态,不能错过这个位置的信息点。

例题

TPO-66/Conversation 1

☞ What was unusual about the conference that the professor attended?

A. It included presentations by many scholars who were not well known to the professor.

B. It included presentations by students.

C. It focused on authors who are respected by most scholars.

D. It focused mostly on less popular literary genres.

文本:

Student: How was that conference last weekend?

Professor: Great. I heard some really terrific presentations, refreshing topics too about authors you don't usually hear too much about.

Student: Why not?

Professor: Oh, well. You know, it's a funny thing about academia. You'd think scholars would do research about every topic imaginable. But actually some authors, some genres aren't respected very much. So not very much is written about them. Uh, Gothic literature, detective novels…

Student: But that's what the conference was about?

Professor: Yeah, pretty much. It was kind of subversive, I guess, but there's a whole wealth of knowledge out there just waiting to be explored. I find that really exciting.

在这段对话中,学生先是问候教授上周末的会议如何,教授就解释了会议的主要内容是关于 some genres aren't respected very much 的,然后题目就针对这个信息点出了第 2 题。

答案　D

TPO-68/Conversation 1

☞ What reason does the student give for missing an appointment with his professor?

A. His alarm clock did not work properly.

B. He was confused about the time of the appointment.

C. He felt ill when he woke up that day.

D. He had an exam in another class.

文本:

Student: Hi, um, I'm Randy Beachham, I really need to speak with Professor Clark right away. Could you get me in to see her?

Administrator: Well, she's conducting oral exams right now, I can't interrupt her. The exams began at 8:00 this morning in her schedule to go on all day.

Student: But I was supposed to take my oral at nine this morning, and, well, don't know what happened. My alarm clock didn't go off for some reason, and I overslept.

Administrator: Oh dear.

在这段话中,学生诉说了自己睡过头的原因且语气着急,提到了闹钟不响的事情,这就是对话开头给出的一个信息点,通常放在第 2 题进行考查。

答案　A

（7）对话的新信息

在托福听力的对话中,到了临近结尾的部分,一般会提出一些新的信息。这些新信息一般会带有明确的时间节点,比如下周、下个学期等。举个例子,关于学生的论文已经结束讨论了,但是教授突然想起来下周有一个展会可能会对学生的论文有所帮助,所以提出展会的事,希望学生去参加。又或者下周让学生交罚款等,都是新信息。

例题

TPO-68/Conversation 2

☞ What does the professor imply she might do about the students paper?

A. Help the student rewrite the conclusion

B. Show it to the writing class professor

C. Consider changing the grade

D. Allow the student to change the topic

文本:

Student:No, I know butterfly migration is different. I wondered why l got such a poor grade. I can rewrite it if you like.

Professor:That's not necessary. Look,now that you've explained things,I'd like to go over your paper again.

Student:OK?

Professor:Let's meet again next week.

在这段话中,学生提出如果需要的话他可以重新写论文,但是教授已经明白他为何会写错结尾,考虑再 go over paper again,下周再见面一次,由此可以根据这个信息点推断出教授已经明白前因后果,考虑重新给学生打分,对应选项 C。

答案　　C

例题

TPO-56/Conversation 2

☞ What information will the woman give the man tomorrow?

A. The cost of the concert tickets

B. The hourly charges for van drivers

C. The amount of money the students need to deposit

D. The amount of money the students still owe

文本：

Employee：Alright. Did you bring the deposit?

Student：Yeah，I did what you suggested asked everybody to give me some money to reserve their space on the bus. They know they'll have to pay more once we know the total is.

Employee：I'll have to run a few numbers to get the final cost. Vans are a lot cheaper than buses but will have to pay for two drivers，they'll charge us by the hour. Of course，you'll get the normal student discount from the van company and I'll deduct your deposit. I can let you know the balance tomorrow.

Student：Great. I'll come by after class.

在这段话中，雇员告诉学生自己会算好所有钱的数额以及明天要带 balance 过来，balance 有余款的意思，这里同时涉及未来的时间点和金钱相关的信息，所以是一个重要的考点，对应答案 D 明天会给学生还需要补多少钱的信息。

答案 D

2. 讲座考点

清晰准确地辨认出讲座(lecture)中的考点信号词是做对题目的第一步。一些刷题较多且对考点掌握比较好的考生往往会发现,有时候,一整篇文章听下来,其实并没有听懂全部,但是考点都抓到了,题目也就自然而然全部做对了。所以应试的终极技巧,就是站在出题者的角度思考,在听音频的过程中,预判考点。

在讲座中往往有十大考点,分别为:并列、解释、因果、转折、举例、比较、强调、问答、否定和态度。

(1) 并列

众所周知,多选题是很多考生的心头"痛",一大部分原因是考生没有很好地意识到听力中的并列考点并且记录下来。

在托福听力当中,广义上的并列有两种形式:局部并列和平行结构。

【经典信号词】

局部并列:and, also, plus, or...

平行结构:another, first, second...

例题

TPO 17/Lecture 4

☞ What two examples does the professor mention to describe the octopus' ability to change its shape? Click on 2 answers.

A. A small round stone

B. The leaves of a plant

C. A cloud of ink

D. A piece of coral

文本：

So it can contract into the shape of a little round stone，and sit perfectly still on the seafloor. Or it can nestle up in the middle of a plant and take the shape of one of the leaves.

本段大背景是在讲章鱼变化形状的能力，从听力中我们可以得知两句话之间由 or 连接，or 前后两个句子中表示形状的核心名词为 stone 和 leaves。那么这两个词就是我们记录的关键，并且有了笔记之后，这道题的答案就非常显而易见了。

答案　AB

TPO10/Lecture1

☞ According to the professor, what three aspects of the Ambulocetus fossil make Ambulocetus a likely bridge between land mammals and sea mammals? Click on 3 answers.

A. It had an elongated skeletal structure.

B. It strongly resembled a modern hippopotamus.

C. It had an unusually kind and thin tail for a whale.

D. It had limbs that could have been used for walking.

E. Its skull had ear bones characteristic of land mammals.

文本：

It clearly had four limbs that couldn't have been used for walking. It also had a long thin tail，typical of mammals，something we don't see in today's whales. But it also had a long skeletal structure，and that long skeletal structure suggests that it was aquatic.

本段大背景是在讲 Ambulocetus fossil 的特点。从音频中可以得知 3 个并列的特点，由 also 连接。因此需要记录下来的内容为 four limbs，tail 和 skeletal structure。

答案　ACD

例题

TPO17/Lecture 4

☞ How does an octopus change color to match the colors in its environment? Click on 2 answers.

A. By raising its papillae

B. By releasing colored ink

C. By reflecting light from its environment

D. By contracting the muscles around its chromatophores

文本：

The color changes are executed by two different kinds of cells in the octopus' skin, mainly by color cells on the skin's surface called chromatophores...

...so that's why the second kind of cell comes in. Just below the chromatophores is a layer of cells that reflect light from the environment，and these cells help the octopus create a precise match with the colors that surround them.

　　本段大背景是在讲章鱼变化颜色的能力，从听力中可以得知章鱼变化颜色的能力由两种细胞控制，并且文章分别详细讲解了两种细胞的作用，采用连接词 mainly 和 second 来引出细胞的类型。因此需要记录下来的内容为 chromatophores 和 reflect light。

　　答案　CD

（2）解释

　　在托福听力讲座中，教授常常会介绍新概念、新事物，讨论新理念，表达新观点。教授通常会用下定义或者解释的方式来引出这些新的专有名词。因此，如果在音频中出现词的解释，那么要记下这个概念，因为这是讲座的重点或难点。

【经典信号词】

- ...are（is）...

- ...means（mean）...

- ...in other words...

- ...namely...

- ...as we know...

- ...are（is）known as...

- ...is called...

- That is why they are called...

- ...refers to...

- ...can be defined as...

- How can we define...?

- The definition of...is...

- By..., I mean...

TPO-49/Lecture 4

☞ What is a skeuomorph?

A. An object with a similar function as another，but with a different design

B. A copy of an object，but made from a different material

C. An exact copy of an object made hundreds of years earlier

D. An object designed to have multiple functions

文本：

However，we have to be careful when it comes to skeuomorphs. These objects are copies of the designs of other objects，but in another material.

　　这段话中，教授通过下定义来解释 skeuomorphs 其实是用不同的材料做出来的一种复制品，因此选 B。

　　答案　　B

(3) 因果

在托福听力考试中,那些带有"因果含义"的词或结构是经常被考查的信息点。在记笔记的时候,还要注意区分哪个信息点是原因、哪个信息点是结果,千万不要混淆。

【经典信号词】

- because/because of
- since
- due to
- on account of
- owing to
- the reason is
- that is why
- so
- hence
- lead to
- result in/resulting from
- as a result
- consequently
- trigger

例题

20160109/Lecture 2

☞ According to the professor, how does the bobtail squid avoid predators?

A. It uses an internal organ to illuminate itself.

B. It uses a symbiotic bacterium to change its color during the day.

C. It only comes out on moonless nights.

D. It stays in shallow areas where its predators cannot swim.

文本：

（Professor）OK，now，let's talk about the bobtail squid.

This squid，I think it's actually even cooler. The bobtail squid have Vibrio fischeri living in them as well. They live in fairly shallow waters in the Pacific Ocean off Hawaii. They're nocturnal so they hide during the day and come out at night.

Now，if you imagine a dark night，the squid blend in fairly well just because it's dark and they're sort of cleanish，translucent. But the problem is they're not translucent enough. So if you have a bright moon，the squid are visible from below by their dark silhouette.

（Male student）And show predators where they are.

（Professor）Exactly! So they develop this special organ where they host Vibrio fischeri. Organ glows just enough to light up the squid so its silhouette becomes as light as the sky and the squid become invisible from below.

答案句出现在因果信号词 so 后面，squid 体内的 Vibrio fischeri 发出的光刚好能照亮乌贼，从下面看不见，这样就能避免被捕食者发现。因此，选项 A 正确。

答案　A

（4）转折

无论是讲座还是听力对话，有转折的地方永远都会有考点。在听力音频中的转折表示方向发生改变，只要有转折就表明说话者要转向另一层含义。转折是对前文的否定，转折后面出现的信息往往是说话者需要突出的内容，因此转折后面的句子多为出题点。

【经典信号词】

• but

• however

• yet

• although

- though

- even though

- despite

- while

- actually

- in fact

- unless

- on the contrary

20160228/Lecture 2

☞ According to the professor, what factors suggest that Gliese 581d might be habitable?

A. Its gravity is strong due to its large mass.

B. It is located in the middle of a habitable zone.

C. Its atmosphere probably has a high carbon dioxide content.

D. Its speed of rotation is almost equal to Earth's.

文本：

(Professor) Gliese 581d orbits around its star called Gliese 581. Because of the planet's large mass, it has seven times the mass of Earth. It's got enough gravity to maintain a dense atmosphere. Some researchers think it might be the first identified exoplanet capable of supporting life.

(Female student) Exoplanet?

(Professor) Yeah, a planet outside our solar system, an exoplanet orbits a star other than our Sun. Gliese 581d was initially dismissed as it's too far from its star and thus too cold to support life. But researchers developed a complex computer program that allowed them to analyze conditions in many possible combinations. And the results were surprising: even though this planet's on the very outer edge of the habitable zone, if it does have a dense mostly carbon dioxide atmosphere，which is likely，it trapped enough heat to partially make up for that distance.

　　音频中说到两个 Gliese 581d 可能适合居住的理由。第一个理由用因果信号词引出，由于这颗行星的质量很大，它的质量是地球的 7 倍，选 A；另一个理由在转折信号词后面，尽管这颗行星位于宜居带的最外缘，但是它很可能有一个以二氧化碳为主的稠密大气层，能够弥补距离问题造成的热量差，选 C。

　　答案　AC

(5) 举例

　　举例考点出现的频率非常高，往往是教授想要通过举例帮助学生理解前面所提到的观点或要点，其对应的题型也基本固定为功能目的题。

　　【经典信号词】

- for example/instance

- take…（for instance）

- think of/about

- in one case

- if

- like/say

　　部分考生可能会感到奇怪，举例除了字面意思上的 for instance、for example 等，还有 if。通过 if，教授讲述的是一个假设性的例子。类似的表达还有 think of sth。所以，考生需要调整对固有的举例的认知，多积累关于举例的信号词。另外，考生的解题思路需要固定下来，例子是为了支持前面提到的观点或者要点，所以要和阅读理解一样"往前找"。思考太多的考生，这个类型的题目往往容易做错。

TPO35/Lecture 1

☞ Why does the professor mention tree roots and rocks?

A. To emphasize the blind mole rat's need for two navigation systems

B. To explain one reason why blind mole rats get lost

C. To give examples of landmarks used by the blind mole rat

D. To describe the materials the blind mole rat uses to build its nest

文本：

Um，one system relies on their sense of time and their ability to remember underground landmarks. For example，let's say a mole rat wants to find its way through its tunnel system back to its nest，where it sleeps. Well，it goes along then feels some hard stones or a tree root under its feet，and it basically says to itself，"OK，here's where I took a left..."

原文的例子中提及了 stone 和 root，而此例子是为了解释说明 the blind mole rat 定位的方式是记住 landmark，选项 C 与原文内容对应，故选项 C 正确。

答案　C

(6) 比较

作比较是托福听力讲座中，教授经常使用的一种讲解方式，特别是当教授比较不同事物或者解释不同理论时。托福听力中的比较考点可以细分为类比和对比两个考点：类比是比较两个事物之间的相同点，对比则是比较两个事物之间的不同点。

【经典信号词】

类比：

• same

• similar

• like

• as

• think of A as B

• imagine B

- resemble

- identical

对比：

- different

- unlike

- not as

- in contrast to

- on the other hand

- 比较级/最高级

20161113/Lecture 1

☞ Why does the professor mention Earth's Great Ocean Conveyor Belt?

A. To compare the flow of gas on Earth and on the Sun

B. To point out a common misconception about sunspots

C. To help students visualize a similar phenomenon on the Sun

D. To point out difference between the magnetic fields of the Sun and Earth

文本：

It turns out that sunspots are moved by a giant circulation system about 200 kilometers below the Sun's surface，a Great Conveyor Belt as we call it. It's actually two belts. See here?

One above the Sun's equator and the other below. And these conveyor belts move the sunspots in a loop，between the solar equator and the poles. Now，remember，there's a similar circulation system here on Earth. It's the Great Ocean Conveyor Belt.

The Great Ocean Conveyor Belt is a network of currents that carry water from ocean to ocean and it controls the weather on Earth. Well，in much the same way the Sun's conveyor belt controls the weather on the Sun. But instead of carrying water，it carries gas. And as the belt moves，it sweeps up，it collects magnetic fields，and it affects the development of future sunspots.

教授先说太阳上有两个 Great Conveyor Belt，后面又讲了地球上也有类似的环流系统叫作 Great Ocean Conveyor Belt。这两个 Belt 虽然很类似，但其实是不一样的，教授对比了这两个 Belt 直接的区别。教授提到地球的 Great Ocean Conveyor Belt 是为了帮助学生理解太阳的 Great Conveyor Belt。因此，选 C。

答案　C

(7) 强调

在托福听力讲座中，教授在讲话的过程中会突出他/她的重点信息，这些被强调的重点信息是考查的一个要点。因此，考生一定要学会如何在一整段音频中抓住教授想要强调突出的重点。强调考点可以分为语气强调和语义强调两种表现形式：语气强调是说话者通过重读、停顿和重复等方式进行强调，语义强调则是说话者用特定词或者句式表达强调。

【经典信号词】

- 轻重音
- 语言节奏改变
- important
- interesting
- especially
- certainly
- just remember
- don't forget
- keep in mind
- and again
- special feature
- one thing I should mention
- be/make sure to…

例题

20160903/Lecture 3

☞ What is the professor's attitude toward the first experiment?

A. She is worried that the participants may have been too distracted to respond accurately.

B. She is not convinced that the same strategy would work in the marketplace.

C. She thinks that using actual products would have added to the validity of the experiment.

D. She thinks it is valuable because it was conducted in a real-world setting.

文本：

So，this first experiment supported the art infusion effect，something about that painting's status as art seem to positively affect the silverware's ratings.

But，what's especially helpful about this experiment is that it was conducted in a crowded restaurant not in a lab. So it basically reproduces the same level of distraction that consumers experience when evaluating actual products in the marketplace. That degree of realism says a lot about the accuracy of these results in my opinion.

这段音频中，教授通过转折信号词 but 引出她要表达的重点内容，在强调信号词 especially 后面说到这次实验是在拥挤的餐厅里进行的，而不是在实验室里。因此，它基本 再现了消费者在评估市场上的实际产品时所经历的同样程度的分心。后面通过重读 realism 和 accuracy 给出自己的态度，在教授看来，这种现实模拟程度在很大程度上说明了 这些结果的准确性。对应选项 D。

答案　D

(8) 问答

问答考点在托福听力的对话和讲座中都可能出现，它的出现在文章中会起到很大作用。

一般来说,在讲座中,问答考点可以分为三种:

第一种,教授提问—学生回答—教授评价:通过互动,引发学生关注。在这种情况中,要格外留意教授的评价环节。一般来说,在教授否定了学生的答案之后,他会给予纠正,因此教授讲解的部分一定要仔细听。

第二种,学生提问—教授回答:解决学生的疑问。在这个环节中,学生通常是有疑问,想要得到教授的解释,教授给出答案后会进一步解释,但在听的过程中不能忘记解释的初衷是解决学生的疑问。

第三种,教授自问自答:引出话题,解决问题。

【经典信号词】

• 疑问句＋答案的组合

例题

20161113/Lecture 4

☞ What does the professor imply about penguins and marine turtles?

A. They cannot stay hydrated by drinking seawater.

B. They mostly live along coastlines and near islands.

C. They spend a lot of time searching for freshwater on land.

D. They can eliminate salt from their bodies without losing much water.

文本:

(Female professor) Now, it might seem strange, but even though many organisms live in the sea, salt water remains a challenging environment for them. It can be difficult for marine organisms to stay hydrated, that is, keep the water content of their bodily fluids within a healthy range. Every animal loses some water over time and, sooner or later, has to replenish it. Drinking seawater to replenish the water content creates a physiological challenge, because by drinking seawater the animal is taking in a lot of salt. And getting salt out of the body is not easy.

(Male student) Isn't that what their, uh, salt gland is for?

(Professor) That's the main mechanism used by, at least, some marine animals like penguins and marine turtles. The special thing about the salt gland is that it secretes the salt in a very concentrated form so there is very little water loss and the animal stays hydrated. Animals that live in the desert，like lizards，they also have salt glands. It's the opposite of the case for most land animals. Most land animals excrete salt in a very diluted form，which means much greater water loss. But，let's take a look at the sea snake.

教授先进行解释，即使许多生物生活在海里，盐水对它们来说仍然是一个具有挑战性的环境。通过饮用海水，动物会摄入大量的盐，而从体内排出盐分并不容易。

学生提问："难道这不是盐腺的作用吗？"

教授回答："至少对于企鹅和海龟等海洋动物来说，盐腺确实起到了这样的作用，盐腺以非常浓缩的形式分泌盐，因此水分损失非常小，动物得以保持它们所需要的水分"。因此选 D。

答案　D

(9) 否定

在托福听力中，否定考点一直是以"隐形大 boss"的形式存在的，这个考点也一直很容易被很多同学忽略。否定考点在语法和阅读等书面表达上出现时会很容易注意到，而在托福听力中出现的时候杀伤力还是比较大的，主要是因为否定考点的变化形式比较多，并伴有一定的语音现象。

【经典信号词】

• not

• 否定前缀：dis-，un-，in-，im-

• 少，没有：never，rarely，barely，few，little，hardly

• 问题缺点：problem，weakness，downside，limitation，restriction，critics，irony

• 语气词：actually，well

例题

20161113/Lecture 4

☞ What did the results of an experiment with sea snakes show?

A. Sea snakes will not drink seawater，even if they are dehydrated.

B. Sea snakes can remain hydrated by drinking both seawater and freshwater.

C. Most species of sea snakes drink only seawater.

D. Sea snakes prefer to swim in freshwater rather than in seawater.

文本：

But it appears that the glands may not be sufficient，or should I say efficient enough to allow the snakes to drink seawater for hydration. Anyway，the researcher wound up taking a group of dehydrated snakes and submerging them in a tank with saltwater. After several hours，he took them out and weighed them to see if they'd gained weight，if they had drunk any of the water. None of them had. He then took the same snakes and put them in a tank of freshwater. All of the snakes immediately began to drink the water. This suggests that although sea snakes have made many adaptations to life in the ocean，drinking seawater is not one of them. They can't drink saltwater. They actually need freshwater to stay hydrated.

　　教授通过运用 although、not、can't、actually 一系列的否定信号词说道，尽管海蛇为适应海洋生活作出了许多改变，但饮用海水并不是其中之一。海蛇不能喝盐水，它们需要淡水来保持水分。因此，选 A。

　　答案　　A

(10) 态度

　　态度考点属于 pragmatic understanding，往往考查考生能否听出说话人对所提及内容的真实看法，是"比较看好""不太看好"，还是"再看看"。搞定态度题的策略分三步走：第一，先发制人。音频中出现态度考点提示的时候就要在笔记中记录,并且明确是哪种态度。第二,火眼金睛。选项中往往会"混入"一些态度方向不符合要求的选项,直接排除。第三,明察秋毫。在剩下的选项中,要仔细辨别一些和原文表述不符或者逻辑错误的选项,加以排除,留下最后的正确答案。

【经典信号词】

- I/We 第一人称表达出现的地方

- 语气发生变化的地方

- 出现明显情感色彩的形容词之处

TPO53/Lecture 1

☞ What is the professor's attitude toward early movie producers?

A. He is critical of their influence on films.

B. He thinks they had little influence on films.

C. He thinks they understood what audiences wanted.

D. He acknowledges that they made progress possible.

文本:

...and this seems a particularly bad idea to us now, one person narrating the action, an early example of a long tradition of movie producers, the ones concerned mostly about making money, not having much confidence in their audience, thinking that people somehow couldn't follow the events otherwise.

在原文中,句子开始的地方有明显的笑声,并且该段落出现了明显的态度词汇"bad idea",明显表达的是否定态度。把握好这一点,就可以立马选出正确答案 A,因为只有选项 A 中的 critical 才符合音频中的情感色彩。

答案 A

第五章　托福真题高频词汇

1. 对话题高频词汇

• 有关"论文"的表达方式

final paper 期末论文

term paper 学期论文

thesis 毕业论文

proposal 开题报告

literature review 文献综述

outline 大纲

catalog 目录

abstract 摘要

topic 话题

keyword 关键词

introduction 引言

subject 主题

theory 理论

note 注释

conclusion 结论

work cited 参考文献

• 选题或修改论文

draft version 草稿

first draft 初稿

final format 终稿

revise 修改

rewrite 重写

narrow down（论文等）缩小范围

broad（论文等）内容宽泛

chosen 精选的

critical thinking 评判性思维

research data 研究数据

scope 范围

collect data 收集数据

plagiarism 抄袭

• 上交或延期交论文或作业

hand in 上交

submit 提交

turn in 提交

due 到期

deadline 最终期限

extension 延期

● 各种考试的说法

mid-term exam 期中考试

final exams 期末考试

take-home exam 拿回家的开卷考试

make up the test 补考

placement test 分班入学考试

● 复习考试或成绩

retake 重修

review 复习

go over the test 复习考试

go through all the questions 复习考试

A minus A−

B plus B+

be all A's and B's 全是 A 和 B

failing grade 不及格分

final grade 最终分数

full marks 满分

GPA 平均积分点

grade mark 分数

high mark 高分

low grade 低分

passing grade 及格分

percentage 百分比

perfect grade 优异成绩

● 其他

beginning students 新生

advanced students 高年级的学生

administer 管理

advantage 优点

application 申请

appraisal 评价；估价

assessment 估价

available 有效的；可用的

book report 读书报告

bulletin board 布告栏

capture the main idea 捕捉主要观点

compare 比较

complete 完成

complicated 复杂的

computer lab 机房

consecutive summer 连续的暑假

cover 封面；封皮

credit is awarded 学分奖励

department 院系

discussion 讨论

essay question 问答题

exam schedule 考试安排表

eye contact 目光接触

gather material 收集资料

homework 作业

include 包含

input 输入

intensive 加强的；集中的；透彻的

interested 感兴趣的

issue 问题；期刊刊号

lab report 实验报告

lack your own ideas 缺少自己的想法

multiple choice question 多选题

office hour 教授与学生面谈的时间

organize 组织

paraphrase 改述

precise statement 明确的陈述

re-reading 重读

handout 课堂讲义

• 课堂讨论

background 背景

research 研究

overwhelmed 不知所措的

investigate 调查；研究

base on 以……为基础

supportive 支持的

subtopic 副主题；小标题

published source 文献

body 正文

play tricks 提弄；恶作剧

assume 假定

hypothesis 猜想

conduct 引导；表现

interpret 解释

clarify 阐明

thought-provoking 发人深省的

comparison 比较

participatory 吸引参与的

improve one's own lives 改善生活质量

make sense 讲得通；明白；理解

observe 观察

diagram 图表；图解

frustrating 令人沮丧的

hydrologic cycle 水循环

recycle 再循环

precipitation 沉淀

evaporation 蒸发

condensation 冷凝

arctic 北极圈；北极的

moisture 湿度

substantial 大量的

summary 概要；摘要

metabolic 新陈代谢的

concentrate on 集中在……

conference 会议

defense 防卫

startle 使……惊吓

dim 昏暗的

manageable 易控制的

identify 鉴定;识别

destructive 有破坏性的

archaeological evidence 考古证据

prehistoric 史前的

harvest 收获

original 原始的;最初的

trauma 创伤

verdict 裁决;定论

sensitivity 敏感性

poisonous 有毒的

crucial 重要的

segment 段;部分

compelling 引人入胜的;令人信服的

specific 特殊的;特定的

artificial 人造的;仿造的

graph 图表

general and casual knowledge 常识性知识

statistical test 统计检验

synthesis 综合;合成

cognitive development 认识发展;认知发展

egocentric 自我中心的;利己主义的

demonstrate 证明;展示;论证

group project 集体项目

fair share 公平分配;公平分享

take credit for 因⋯⋯得到好评;把⋯⋯归功于

candidate 候选人;候补者;应试者

undergraduate research fund 大学研究基金会

in-depth research 深入研究

application 应用;请求

research equipment 科研设备

eligible 合格的;合适的;符合条件的;有资格当选的

relevance 相关性

linguistics project 语言学项目

• 关于"选课"的表达方式

take 选课

enroll 选课

• "退课"的各种说法

drop 退课

get out of 退课

• 学科名称

accounting 会计学

anatomy 解剖学

anthropology 人类学

archaeology 考古学

architecture 建筑学

arts 文科

astronomy 天文学

biology 生物学

botany 植物学

chemistry 化学

computer science 计算机科学

ecology 生态学

economics 经济学

electronics 电子学

engineering 工科

geology 地质学

geography 地理学

history 历史学

linguistics 语言学

math 数学

oceanography 海洋学

philosophy 哲学

physics 物理

psychology 心理学

science 理科

topography 地形学

statistic 统计学

zoology 动物学

· 课程种类

major 主修

minor 副修

introductory 初级课

preparatory course 预备课

the beginning course 初级课程

intermediate course 中级课

advanced course 高级课

prerequisite 先修课程

required course 必修课

selective elective 选修课

summer session 暑期课程

credit course 学分课程

graduate course 研究生课程

workshop 专题小组

seminar 高级研讨性课程

quarter 小学期；季度

· 教学相关名词

associate 同事；副手

lecture hall 报告厅

regular meeting 例会

access 方法

attendance 出勤

challenging 有挑战的

class participation 课堂参与

counselor 咨询者；顾问

course guideline 课程纲要

decision 决定

distance education 远程教育

enquiry 询问

excellent reputation 好的声誉

extra time 额外时间

fixed date 固定日期

instructor 讲师

lecturer 讲师

off-campus 校外

openings 可供注册的名额

president 大学校长

print materials 打印材料

program 课程；项目

qualified 合格的

quite a heavy load 负担沉重

rehearsal 彩排

remote 远程的

requirement 要求

research assistant 助研

rough 糟糕的；困难的

semester 学期

signature 签字

skip class 逃课

syllabus 教学大纲

prerequisite 先决条件

teaching assistant 助教

• 迟到旷课场景

miss class 缺席

point out 指出

chapter 章节

divide 划分

project 课题

show up 露面；出席

attend 出席；参加

admission 免费入场

emergency 紧急情况

make sense 讲得通；理解；明白

• 转学场景

transfer 转学

public university 公立大学

private university 私立大学

community college 社区大学

reputation 声誉

class size 班级规模

interact 互动

group discussion 小组讨论

afford 支付得起

affordable 担负得起的

location 位置

environment 环境

top student 优等生；高材生

application 申请

special 特殊的

• 图书馆各区域

library 图书馆

front desk 前台

video library 录像图书馆

reference section 参考书区域

stacks 书库

circulation desk 借书处

periodical reading room 期刊阅览室

secondhand bookstore 二手书店

delivery 借书台

information desk 服务台

photocopy room 复印室

shelf 书架

• 借与还

check out 办理(借、还)手续

renew 续借

reserve 预留;贮藏

recall 召回

librarian 图书管理员

library card 借书证

loan period 借书期限

overdue 过期

overdue fine 过期罚金

suspend 延缓;推迟

interlibrary loan service 馆际互借服务

privilege 特权

• 图书馆查文献

electronic and printed version 电子版和印
    刷版

photocopier 影印机

list by title 根据标题列出

literature review 文献综述

magazine 杂志

periodical 期刊

publication 出版物

contemporary review 当代评论

database 数据库

article 文章

alphabetic index 按字母顺序排列的索引

by author and by topic 根据作者主题列出

call number 图书编目号码

focus 关注

front cover 封面;封皮

dictionary 字典

inscription 题词;铭文

title index 书目索引

video tape 录像带

• 书店

merchandise 商品

refund 退款

purchase 买

retreat 退书

buy-back 回购

• 学位及求职材料

intern 实习生

bachelor degree 学士学位

master degree 硕士学位

doctor degree 博士学位

Ph.D 博士学位

graduate certificate 毕业证书

resume 简历

recommendation letter 推荐信

diploma 文凭

• 应聘

recruit 招聘

career 职业；事业

wear a suit 穿正装

interview 面试

firm 公司

advancement 晋升

• 关于薪水

payroll 工资单

salary 工资

bank account 银行账户

credit card 信用卡

deposit 存款

• 关于辞职

quit 辞职

fire 开除

• 校园各种职位

university president 大学校长

department secretary 院系秘书

dean 院长

registrar 登记员

counselor 顾问

tutor 辅导老师

instructor 辅导老师

advisor 指导老师

director 导师；系主任

supervisor 导师

lecturer 讲师

receptionist 接待员

consultant 顾问

clerk 职员

employee 雇员

staff 职员

• 项目

survey 问卷调查

experiment 实验

interfere 影响

observation 观察报告

analyze data 分析数据

interpret data 解释数据

• 入学

enrollment 登记；注册

opening ceremony 开业典礼；仪式

commencement ceremony 毕业典礼

orientation meeting 开学说明会

freshman（大学）一年级学生

sophomore（大学）二年级学生

junior（大学）三年级学生

senior 毕业班学生

underground 本科

graduate 研究生课程

average 平均的；一般的

below average 低于平均水平的；差的

canteen 餐厅

administration building 行政大楼

main building 主楼

teaching building 教学楼

dormitory 宿舍

auditorium 会堂；礼堂

dining hall 食堂

• 关于"钱"

financial aid 经济援助

scholarship 奖学金

tuition 学费

grant 助学金

loan 贷款

donation 捐助

sponsor 赞助

• 校外活动

competitive 竞争的

benefit future career 有益于未来的职业

field research 田野调查

babysitter 临时照顾幼儿者

qualification 资格；合格的

research assistantship 研究奖学金

student union 学生会

club 俱乐部

membership 成员资格

career service 职业指导

summer break 暑假

practice 练习

volunteer 志愿者

tough 艰苦的；困难的

stressed 压力大的

balance 平衡

get through 通过

fondness 爱好；溺爱

announcement 公告

fill out an application 填写申请表

responsible for 对……负责

career training 职业培训

housing and food allowance 食宿津贴

internship program 实习项目

working experience 工作经验

flyer 传单

poster 海报

full-time 全职

part-time 兼职

academic credit 学分

supervise 监督；管理；指导

handout 政府拨款；捐赠品

hand out 分发

career advisory service 职业咨询服务

financial aid 经济援助

teaching assistantship 助教奖学金

living expense 生活费

vacation 假期

weather 天气;露天的;风化

• 体育运动

marathon 马拉松

motivator 动力

back into shape 塑型;恢复身材

inspire 鼓励

running buddies 跑步的伙伴

positive 积极的

campus daily 校园日常生活

ceremony 典礼

alumni 校友会

regular hobby 一般嗜好

physical fitness routine 常规体能锻炼

bicyclist 骑脚踏车的人

expert riders 熟练的骑手

endurance test 忍耐力测试

racers 比赛者

safety 安全

physical education class 体育课

rock climbing 攀岩

rope 绳

belt 带子

buckle 扣住

safety equipment 安全设备

climbing trip 攀岩

break 休息;打破;突变

rock concert 摇滚音乐会

• 食宿

accommodation 住所;膳宿

studio 工作室;独立套间

home-stay 寄宿家庭

roommate 同居者;室友

lease 租借;租约

rent 租金

single room 单人房

twin room 双人房

two-bedroom apartment 两居室

pillow 枕头

sheet 被单

mattress 床垫

blanket 毯子

towel 手巾;毛巾

quilt 棉被

electric appliance 家用电器

instrument 电器

heater 加热器;炉子

heating unit 暖气片

air conditioner 空调设备

stove 炉子

microwave oven 微波炉

washer 洗衣机;烘干机

laundry 洗衣店

oven 烤箱；烤炉

range 炉灶

dishwasher 洗碗机

heater 热水器

coffeepot 咖啡壶

refrigerator 冰箱

vacuum cleaner 吸尘器

laundromat 自助洗衣店

maintenance 维修；保养

furniture 家具

bookshelf 书架

bookcase 书柜

couch 沙发

chest 柜子；橱；箱子

cabinet (电视机等)机箱；储藏柜；陈列柜

cupboard 碗橱

carpet 地毯

curtain 窗帘

furnishings 室内陈设

possessions 个人财产

get insurance for personal possessions 个人
    财产保险

garbage 垃圾

dispose 处理

leaking 泄露

dorm 宿舍

hygienic 卫生的；保健的；卫生学的

unsanitary 不卫生的；有碍健康的

chaotic 混沌的；混沌的；无秩序的

messy 凌乱的；散乱的；肮脏的

sink 水槽

pipe 管理

shutter 快门；百叶窗

• 关于食堂

restaurant 餐厅

organic food 有机食物

deep fried food 油炸食物

snack 小吃；快餐

salad 沙拉

waitress 女服务员

waiter 男服务员

auditorium 礼堂；会堂

2. 讲座题高频词汇

• Art 艺术

fine arts 美术

oil painting 油画

watercolor 水彩画

tempera 蛋彩画

sketch 速写；素描

pastel 彩色蜡笔画

pastel drawing 彩粉画

poster 海报；招贴画

charcoal drawing 木炭画

fresco 壁画

engraving 版画

lithograph 石板画

landscape painting 风景画

still life 静物画

portrait 肖像画

panorama 全景画

caricature 漫画

animator 漫画家

dye 染；染色

pigment 颜色；色素

indigo 靛蓝

canvas 油画布

brush 画笔

drawing board 画板

brushstroke 绘画技巧；笔画

perspective 透视画法

paste 裱糊

charcoal 木炭笔；木炭

calligraphy 书法

sculpture 雕塑

statue 塑像

sculptor 雕塑家

figurine 小雕像

bust 半身雕塑像

original 原作

autograph 真迹

replica 复制品

keyboard instrument 键盘乐器

percussion 打击乐器组

string music 弦乐

wind music 管乐

pluck 弹（乐器）

violin 小提琴

viola 中提琴

cello 大提琴

harp 竖琴

harpsichord 大键琴

organ 风琴

horn 号；喇叭

clarinet 单簧管

oboe 双簧管

folk music 民间音乐

classical music 古典音乐

symphony 交响乐

orchestra （管弦）乐队

choir 合唱团；唱诗班

quartet 四重奏

note 音符

score 乐谱

movement 乐章

quality 音质

volume 音量

pitch 音高

chord 和弦

harmony 和声

rest 休止

time 节拍

vocal music 声乐

lyric 歌词

rhythm 旋律；节奏

melody 曲子；曲调

conduct 指挥

podium 指挥台

accompaniment 伴奏

fanatical 狂热的

lullaby 催眠曲

narrative prose 叙述性散文

descriptive prose 描写性散文

satirist 讽刺作家

biographer 传记作家

prose 散文

autobiography 自传

poet 诗人

poetry 诗歌；诗学

poem 诗

ballad 民谣

fiction 小说

allegory 寓言

fairy tale 童话

legend 传说

proverb 谚语

myth 神话

mythical 神话的；虚构的

mythology 神话学；神话的总称

model（人物）原型

leading character 主人公

literary criticism 文学批评

literary studies 文学研究

school of literature 文学流派

genre 类型；流派；风格；体裁

comparative literature 比较文学

realism 现实主义

surrealism 超现实主义

futurism 未来主义

modernism 现代主义

minimalist 简单抽象派艺术家

choreographer 舞蹈编排家

feminist 女权主义者

humanitarian 人道主义者

philanthropist 慈善家

proprietor 业主

mortal 凡人

figurehead 名誉领袖

disciple 学徒

apprentice 学徒

avant-garde 前卫派

symbolic 象征性的

eccentric 古怪的

erratic 奇怪的

romantic 浪漫的

spare 简朴的

immortal 不朽的

classic 经典的

posthumous 死后(出版)的

clumsy 笨拙的

innocent 天真的;无罪的

emotive 感人的

sentimental 感伤的;多愁善感的

cheerless 无精打采的;无生命力的

nostalgia 怀旧主义;思乡

lovelorn 相思病的

prodigious 巨大的

photographer 摄影家

snapshot 快照

develop 冲洗(照片)

enlarge 放大

foreground 前景

background 背景

high definition 高清晰度

exposure 曝光

instant camera 拍立得;一次成像相机

camera lens 相机镜头

long focus lens 长镜头

tripod 三脚架

filter 滤色镜

dark room 暗室

close-up 特写

out of focus 调焦不准

architecture 建筑学

architect 建筑学家

wing 副楼;侧楼

log structure 原木结构

metal-frame 金属结构

skyscraper 摩天大楼

planetarium 天文馆

aquarium 水族馆

archive 档案馆

cathedral 大教堂

mosque 清真寺

the Triumphal Arch 凯旋门

sphinx 狮身人面像

pyramid 金字塔

the Statue of Liberty 自由女神像

pantomime 哑剧;童话剧

acrobatics 杂技

ballerina 芭蕾舞女

tunic 束腰外衣

textile 纺织品;纺织工艺;纺织原料

fibre 纤维;细丝

• Zoology 动物学

creature 生物

organism 生物

micro-organism 微生物

zoology 动物学

paleontology 古生物学

paleontologist 古生物学家

extinction 灭绝

endangered species 濒危物种

marine 海洋的

genetics 遗传学	herbivorous 食草的
Darwinism 达尔文学说	omnivorous 杂食的
survival of the fittest 适者生存	mammal 哺乳动物
natural selection 自然选择	homeotherm 恒温动物
anatomy 解剖学	cold-blooded animal 冷血动物
specimen 标本	poikilotherm 变温动物
tissue 组织	symbiosis 共生现象
niche 小生态环境	solitary 独居的
phylum（表示生物分类的)门	gregarious 群居的
class 纲	habitat 栖息地
order 目	burrow 洞穴；藏身处
suborder 亚目	predator 捕食者
family 科	prey 捕食
genus 属	forage 觅食
fauna 动物群	respire 呼吸
invertebrate 无脊椎动物	camouflage 伪装
vertebrate 脊椎动物	hibernate 冬眠；蛰伏
aquatic life 水生生物	migrate 迁移
reptile 爬行动物	mate 配偶；交配
amphibian 两栖动物	fertilize 使……受精
rodent 啮齿动物	incubate 孵化
ruminant 反刍动物	spawn（鱼、虾、蛙等)孵
parasitic animal 寄生动物	hatch（鸟等)孵
primate 灵长动物	breed 品种；繁殖
plankton 浮游生物	multiply 繁殖
mollusk 软体动物	reproduce 繁殖
herbivore 食草动物	regenerate 再生
scavenger 食腐动物	genetic 遗传的；基因的
carnivorous 食肉的	mutate 变异；产生突变

chirp（鸟、虫）叫声

squeak（老鼠等）吱吱叫

sting 针；刺；白蜇

metamorphosis 变形

molt 脱毛

horde（昆虫等）群

swarm（昆虫等）群

flock（牛、羊等）群

herd 兽群

scale 鳞

feather 羽毛

furry 毛皮的；毛皮制的

armor 甲

spinal cord 脊椎

digestive system 消化系统

excretory system 排泄系统

reproductive system 生殖系统

circulatory system 循环系统

respiratory system 呼吸系统

hormonal system 内分泌系统

digestive duct 消化管

digestive gland 消化腺

stomach 胃

intestine 肠

salivary gland 唾液腺

liver 肝

enzyme 酶

fodder 饲料

fowl 家禽

livestock 家畜，牲畜

cowshed 牛棚

pigpen 猪舍

poultry 家禽

graze 放牧

jellyfish 水母

coral 珊瑚

dolphin 海豚

shrimp 小虾

prawn 对虾

lobster 龙虾

crab 螃蟹

mussel 贻贝；蚌类

clam 蛤；蛤蜊

oyster 牡蛎；蚝

starfish 海星

squid 鱿鱼；乌贼

octopus 章鱼

squirrel 松鼠

marten 貂

bat 蝙蝠

otter 水獭

antelope 羚羊

bison 野牛

gorilla 大猩猩

chimpanzee 黑猩猩

baboon 狒狒

beaver 海狸

elk 麋鹿

reindeer 驯鹿

giraffe 长颈鹿

rhinoceros 犀牛

hippopotamus 河马

dinosaur 恐龙

sloth 树懒

buffalo 非洲野牛

turtle 龟

lizard 蜥蜴

chameleon 变色龙

crocodile 鳄鱼

toad 蟾蜍;癞蛤蟆

ornithology 鸟类学

robin 知更鸟

owl 猫头鹰

penguin 企鹅

crane 鹤

plumage 翅膀;鸟类羽毛

bill（鸟）嘴

beak（鹰等的）嘴

claw 爪子

insect 昆虫

pest 害虫

grasshopper 蚱蜢

wasp 黄蜂

spider 蜘蛛

worm 虫;蠕虫

larva 幼虫

caterpillar 毛虫

nit 幼虫;卵

bug 虫子;电脑中程序错误

hopper 跳虫（跳蚤）;单足跳者

finch 雀

moth 飞蛾

cricket 蟋蟀

venom 毒液

venomous 有毒的

hive 蜂巢

heredity 遗传

domesticate 驯养;驯化

• Botany 植物学

vegetative 植物的;植被的;无性繁殖的

botany 植物学

botanical 植物学的

horticulture 园艺学

morphology 形态学

nucleus 细胞核

cell wall 细胞壁

perennial 多年一生的

annual 一年一生的

jungle 丛林

lawn 草坪

meadow 草地;牧场

prairie 大草原

tundra 冻原

marsh 沼泽

swamp 沼泽

ranch 大农场

cluster 一簇(灌木)

fern 蕨类植物

moss 苔藓

lichen 地衣,苔藓

shrub 灌木

bush 灌木

algae 海藻

tissue 组织

canopy 树冠层;顶棚

foliage 叶

leaflet 小叶

rosette (叶的)丛生

decompose 分解;使……腐烂

disintegrate 分解

stem 茎

bulb 球茎

stalk 杆

sprout 嫩芽;抽枝

skin 果皮

shell 果壳

kernel 果仁

flesh 果肉

husk 壳;外皮

trunk 树干

bark 树皮

branch 树枝

bough 大或者粗的树枝

twig 小树枝

resin 树脂;松脂

herb 药草;香草

herbicide 除草剂

blossom 花;开花

bud 花蕾

petal 花瓣

nectar 花蜜

column 花柱

pollen 花粉

pollinate 传授花粉

aroma 香气;芳香

evergreen 常青树

conifer tree 针叶树

pine 松树

orchid 兰花

lily 百合

violet 紫罗兰

jasmine 茉莉花

cactus 仙人掌

tulip 郁金香

amber 琥珀

citric 柠檬的;采自柠檬的

chlorophyll 叶绿素

photosynthesis 光合作用

chemosynthesis 化合作用

metabolism 新陈代谢

nutrition 营养

malnourished 营养不良的

nourish 施肥于……;滋养

wither 凋谢

shrivel 枯萎;干枯

carbohydrate 碳水化合物

glucose 葡萄糖

starch 淀粉

protein 蛋白质

vitamin 维生素

cross-breed 杂交

immunology 免疫学

immunity 免疫

vaccine 疫苗

antibody 抗体

microorganism 微生物

microbe 微生物

microscopic 精微的;微小的

toxin 毒素

virus 病毒

disinfect 消毒

sterilization 灭菌

fungus 真菌

fungi (pl.)真菌

yeast 酵母

bacteria 细菌

ferment 发酵

infection 传染;感染

penicillin 青霉素

amino acid 氨基酸

chromosome 染色体

oxidation 氧化

sanitation 卫生

ecology 生态学

ecosystem 生态系统

bio-diversity 生物多样性

mutation 变异

flora 植物群

food chain 食物链

balance of nature 自然界生态平衡

tropic rain forest 热带雨林

agriculture 农业

agricultural 农业的

aquaculture 水产业

husbandry 农事;耕作

hydroponics 水耕法;水栽培

arable 可耕的

irrigate 灌溉

tractor 拖拉机

silt 淤泥

weed 野草;除草

pasture 牧地

plantation 耕地;种植园

seedbed 苗床

orchard 果园

barn 谷仓

cotton 棉花

garlic 大蒜

lettuce 莴苣

wheat 小麦

barley 大麦

oat 燕麦

spinach 菠菜

indigenous 本土的

hay 干草

fertilizer 肥料

fertile 肥沃的

harvest 收获

prolific 多产的，丰富

• Archaeology 考古学

archaeology 考古学

archaeologist 考古学家

anthropology 人类学

anthropologist 人类学家

hominid 原始人类；人科的

homogeneous 同一种族（种类）的

heterogeneous 不同种族的

chronological 按年代顺序排列的

the Stone Age 石器时代

he Bronze Age 青铜器时代

the Iron Age 铁器时代

Paleolithic 旧石器时代的

Mesolithic 中石器时代的

Neolithic 新石器时代的

prehistoric 史前的

tribe 部落

clan 氏族

excavation 挖掘

excavate 挖掘

unearth 挖掘

ruin 遗迹；废墟

remain 遗产；遗骸

relic 遗物；文物

artifact 手工艺品

antique 古物；古董

erode 腐蚀

corrode 腐蚀

decay 腐烂；衰败

weather 风化；使……风化

antiquity 古代；古老

porcelain 瓷器

skull 颅骨

cranial 颅骨的

cave man 山顶洞人

rock painting 岩画

scoop 铲子

gear 齿轮

hammer 锤子；铁锤

• Earth Science 地球科学

geography 地理

gravity 地心引力；重力

hemisphere 半球

meridian 子午线；经线

parallel 纬线；平行圈

latitude 纬度

longitude 经度

elevation 海拔

altitude 高度;海拔

horizon 地平线

equator 赤道

temperate 温带的

temperate latitudes 温带地区

tropic 热带

tropical 热带的

frigid 寒带的

Arctic 北极的;北极区的

the North Pole 北极

the Arctic Circle 北极圈

Antarctic 南极的;南极区的

the South Pole 南极

the Antarctic Circle 南极圈

Antarctica 南极洲

aurora 极光

crust 地壳

mantle 地幔

core 地核

continental crust 大陆地壳

oceanic crust 海洋地壳

layer 地层

stratum 地层

strata（pl.）地层

stratigraphy 地层学

fault 断层

fault plane 断层面

fault zone 断层带

rift 断裂

split 断裂

terrain 地域

landlocked area 内陆

inland waterway 内陆河

subcontinent 次大陆

continental shelf 大陆架

transcontinental 横贯大陆的

topography 地形学

topographical 地形学的

plateau 高地

zenith 顶点;顶峰

sector 扇形面;地区

upland 丘陵;高地;丘陵的,高地的

lowland 低地

basin 盆地

oasis 绿洲

enclave 被外国领地包围的土地

canyon 峡谷

gorge 峡谷

channel 海峡

strait 海峡

gulf 海湾;鸿沟;隔阂

ridge 山脊;分水岭

cliff 山崖

precipitous 陡峭的

valley 山谷

hillside 山坡

dune 沙丘

cavern 洞穴

subterranean 地底下

continental island 大陆岛

volcanic island 火山岛

coral island 珊瑚岛

islet 小岛

peninsular 半岛的

coastline 海岸线

watershed 分水岭

upper reaches 上游

lower reaches 下游

tributary 支流

fountain 泉水

riverbed 河床

bay 海湾

waterfall 瀑布

reef 暗礁

coral reef 珊瑚礁

tide 潮汐

torrent 水的急流

terrestrial 地球的；陆地的

terrestrial heat 地热

terrestrial magnetism 地磁

geothermal 地热

continental drift 大陆漂移学说

sea-floor spreading 海床扩展

evaporate 蒸发

salinity 含盐度

saline 盐的；含盐分的

salty 含盐的

ocean bottom 海床

sediment 沉积物

lithosphere 岩石圈

bedrock 岩床；基础；根底

fieldstone 散石；大卵石

pebble 鹅卵石

igneous rocks 火成岩

sedimentary rocks 沉积岩

metamorphic rocks 变质岩

limestone 石灰岩

granite 花岗岩

marble 大理石

gem 宝石

diamond 钻石

emerald 绿宝石

ruby 红宝石

quartz 石英

obsidian 黑曜石

sandstone 砂岩

mineral 矿物

mineralize 使……矿物化

ore 矿石

rubble 碎石

iron 铁

platinum 白金；铂金

silver 银

bronze 青铜	El Nino 厄尔尼诺现象
copper 黄铜	noxious 有毒的
aluminum 铝	fume（有毒的）废气
tin 锡	waste 废物
lead 铅	sewage disposal 污水处理
zinc 锌	geology 地质学
nickel 镍	lagoon 咸水湖
mercury 汞；水银	hot spring 温泉
sodium 钠	topsoil 表层土
the Mediterranean Sea 地中海	aquifer 蓄水层
Pompeii 庞贝（古城）	brook 小河
the Grand Canyon 大峡谷	sinuous 蜿蜒迂回的
the Nile River 尼罗河	ford 浅滩
resource 资源	watercourse 水道
fossil fuel 矿物燃料	seaport 海港；港口
energy conservation 能源保护	tectonic plates 地壳构造板块
solar energy 太阳能	continental margin 大陆边缘
tidal energy 潮汐能	subduction 俯冲
fuel-efficient 节能型的	bulge 凸起物
renewable 可再生的	glacier 冰川
greenhouse 温室	glacial 冰川的
acid rain 酸雨	glacial epoch 冰川期
infrared radiation 红外线辐射	glacial drift 冰碛
ozone layer 臭氧层	iceberg 冰山
ultraviolet radiation 紫外辐射	active volcano 活火山
air pollution 空气污染	extinct volcano 死火山
water pollution 水污染	dormant volcano 休眠火山
deforestation 滥伐森林	shield volcano 盾状火山（较平缓）
desertification 沙漠化	cone volcano 锥状火山（较陡峭）

erupt 火山喷发

crater 火山口

lava（火山喷发后外部形成的）熔岩

magma（火山未喷发时内部的）岩浆

volcanic dust 火山尘

volcanic ash 火山灰

earthquake/quake/tremor/seism 地震

seismic 地震的

seismology 地震学

magnitude 震级

seismic intensity scale 地震强度分级

seismic wave 地震波

transverse wave 横波

longitudinal wave 纵波

epicenter 震中

epicentral distance 震中距

aftershock 余震

cataclysm 灾变

tsunami 海啸

ebb 退潮；衰退

undersea landslide 海底山崩

global warming 全球变暖

ledge 矿层；矿脉

smelt 冶炼

bonanza 富矿带

• Astronomy 天文学

astronomy 天文学

astronomical observatory 天文台

astrophysics 天文物理学

astrology 占星学

pseudoscience 伪科学

cosmos 宇宙

universe 宇宙

cosmology 宇宙哲学；宇宙论

cosmic 宇宙的

celestial 天的，天体的

celestial body 天体

heavenly body 天体

celestial sphere 天球

dwarf 矮星

the Milky Way 银河系

galaxy 银河系

intergalactic 星系间的

nebula 星云

star cluster 星团

supernova 超新星

solar system 太阳系

solar corona 日冕

solar eclipse 日食

constellation 星座

the Big Dipper 北斗七星

star 恒星

stellar 恒星的

interstellar 恒星间的

planet 行星

interplanetary 行星间的

planetoid 微型行星

asteroid 小行星

satellite 卫星

comet 彗星

meteoroid 流星体

meteor 流星

meteorite 陨石

meteor shower 流星雨

Earth 地球

Mars 火星

Venus 金星

Saturn 土星

Jupiter 木星

Mercury 水星

Uranus 天王星

Neptune 海王星

Pluto 冥王星

orbit 轨道

revolve 旋转

spin 旋转

rotate 自转

rotation 自转

revolve 公转

revolution 公转

oval 椭圆的

elliptical 椭圆的

round 圆的

circular 圆的

lunar 月球的;阴历的

solar calendar 阳历

lunar calendar 阴历;农历

leap year 闰年

photosphere 光球;光球层

chromosphere 色球;色球层

sunspot 太阳黑子(发生在光球层)

flare 耀斑(发生在色球层)

outer space 太空;外层空间

spacecraft 宇宙飞船

spaceship 宇宙飞船

space shuttle 航天飞机

space telescope 空间望远镜

remote-sensing 遥感的

spaceman 宇航员

astronaut 宇航员

space suit 宇航服

space debris 太空垃圾

interferometer 干扰仪;干涉仪

black hole 黑洞

luminosity 光度

light year 光年

centrifugal force 离心力

centripetal force 向心力

international date line 国际日期变更线

• Meteorology 气象学

meteorology 气象学

meteorologist 气象学家

climate 气候

seasonality 季节性

atmosphere 大气层

troposphere 对流层

stratosphere 平流层

cold front 冷锋

warm air mass 热气团

tropical depression 热带低气压

current（气）流

moisture 潮湿，水气

moist 潮湿的

damp 潮湿的

humid 潮湿的

humidity 湿度

saturate 饱和

meteorological station 气象站

forecast 预报

barometer 气压计

spell 一段时间

vapor 蒸汽

evaporate 蒸发

dew 露

frost 霜

fog 雾

mist 雾

smog 烟雾

chilly 寒冷的

droplet 小水滴

condense 浓缩

crystal 水晶体

crystallize 结晶

blast 一阵

downpour 大雨

torrential（大雨）倾盆的；猛烈的

tempest 暴风雨

drizzle 细雨；卜毛毛雨

shower 阵雨

hail 冰雹；下冰雹

blizzard 暴风雪

snowstorm 暴风雪

avalanche 雪崩

snow slide 雪崩

precipitation（雨、露、雪等）降水

thunder 雷

lightning 闪电

breeze 微风；吹微风

sandstorm 沙暴

dust storm 尘暴

monsoon 季风

gale 大风

whirlwind 旋风

typhoon 台风

hurricane 飓风

tornado 龙卷风

twister 龙卷风

cyclone 龙卷风

wind scale 风级

wind velocity 风速

wind direction 风向

funnel 漏斗云

catastrophe 灾难

devastation 破坏

submerge 淹没

drought 旱灾

balmy 温和的

tepid adj. 微温的

• Physics & Chemistry 物理与化学

organic chemistry 有机化学

inorganic chemistry 无机化学

biochemistry 生物化学

chemist 化学家;药剂师

alchemy 炼金术

microscope 显微镜

microscopic 用显微镜可见的

sensitivity 灵敏度

test tube 试管

reagent 试剂

solution 溶液

solvent 溶剂

dissolve 溶解

soluble 可溶的

solidify 固化

liquefy 液化

gasify 气化

vaporize 汽化

dilution 稀释

distillation 蒸馏

element 化学元素

oxygen 氧气

oxide 氧化物

hydrogen 氢气

nitrogen 氮气

helium 氦气

ammonia 氨气

methane 沼气

carbon 碳

hydrocarbon 碳氢化合物

calcium 钙

silicon 硅

iodine 碘

uranium 铀

zircon 锆石

petroleum 石油

carbon dioxide 二氧化碳

carbonic acid 碳酸

sulfur 硫

sulfide 硫化物

sulfuric acid 硫酸

isotope 同位素

compound 化合物

physics 物理学

atom 原子

nucleus 原子核

electron 电子

neutron 中子

proton 质子

molecule 分子

particle 粒子

ion 离子

volt 伏特

voltage 电压

uniform motion 匀速运动

acceleration 加速度

deceleration 减速度

gravitation 引力

relativity 相对

acceleration of gravity 重力加速度

conservation of energy 能量守恒

mechanics 力学

power 功率

acoustics 声学

reflection 反射

refraction 折射

resonance 共振

reverberation 反射;回响

ultrasonic 超声波

conduction 传导

electrode 电极

direct current 直流电

magnet 磁铁

magnetism 磁学

magnetic force 磁力

optics 光学

combustion 燃烧

tangential 切线的;正切的;相切的

spectrum 频谱;光谱

spectroscopy 光谱学

X ray X 射线

Gamma ray γ 射线

• Sociology 社会学

constitution 宪法

legislation 立法

Democrat 民主党

Republican 共和党

Amendment 修正案

Congress 美国国会

Senate 参议院

House of Representatives 众议院

monarchy 君主制

anarchism 无政府主义

federal system 联邦制

presidential system 总统制

tariff 关税

immigrant 移民

veto 否决

the War of American Independence 美国独
立战争

the American Civil War 美国内战

subsistence 存活;生活

commodity 商品

bank loan 银行贷款

interest 利息

withdraw（从银行账户中）提款

payroll 发薪名单；薪水总额

paycheck 薪水；付薪水的支票

the Great Depression 大萧条

kinship 亲属关系；血缘关系

consumerism 消费主义；保护消费者权益
   主义

metropolis 国际大都市

congestion 拥堵

poverty 贫穷

welfare 福利

amenity 舒适；适意

infrastructure 基础设施

CBD（Central Business District）中央商业区

urban sprawl（盲目的）城市开发

exorbitant 过度的；昂贵的

migration 移民；移居

nomadic 游牧的；流浪的

depopulation 人口减少

spiritual 心灵的

conformity 从众

majority 多数人

minority 少数人

第六章　托福笔记符号推荐

关于笔记,每位考生可以形成一套自己的笔记模式,自己用得顺手,方便记录就可以。当然有一部分考生可能刚刚接触托福考试,对于用什么样的符号来记录毫无头绪。还有的考生,为了不遗漏重要信息,整句整句听写句子。这样的做法不但没有把要点记录下来,反而有可能因为记笔记而分神,导致未能理解文章的内容。记住,千万不要为了记笔记而记笔记,要科学简便地记录重要信息。

本书整理了一些简单好记的笔记符号,可供考生参考。除了利用符号以外,考生还要学会中英文结合或者字母简写的方法,以达到快速记录的效果。比如"water"这个词,与其写下英文,不如直接写"水"这个汉字来得快。再如"background"这个较长的词,完全可以简写成"bkg"来节省时间。

当然,关于记笔记,不同的老师有不同的看法。有的老师觉得无需记笔记,全部听懂题就做出来了。这种做法仅适用于记忆力非常好且能够完全理解文章的考生。关于记笔记的作用,在这里强调几点:首先,记笔记可以加深考生对考点的印象,如果考点被识别出来,并且记在大脑里,做题的时候不看笔记也可以;其次,记笔记能够有效避免遗漏或记混一些细节信息;最后,在记笔记的过程中,大脑在思考,从而有利于注意力集中,不会听着听着就走神。

托福笔记符号见表6.1。

表 6.1 托福笔记符号

含 义	符 号
主旨	☆
转折	△
否定	X
强调	！（数量越多强调越明显）
问答	？
因为	∵
所以	∴
肯定	√
类比	≈
对比	△
并列	+
举例	eg
人名/地名等	首字母大写
态度	！（数量越多态度越强烈）
上升/下降	↑/↓
相同	=
解释	i.e
交换	∞